D0116473

THE SQUIRE'S BRIDE

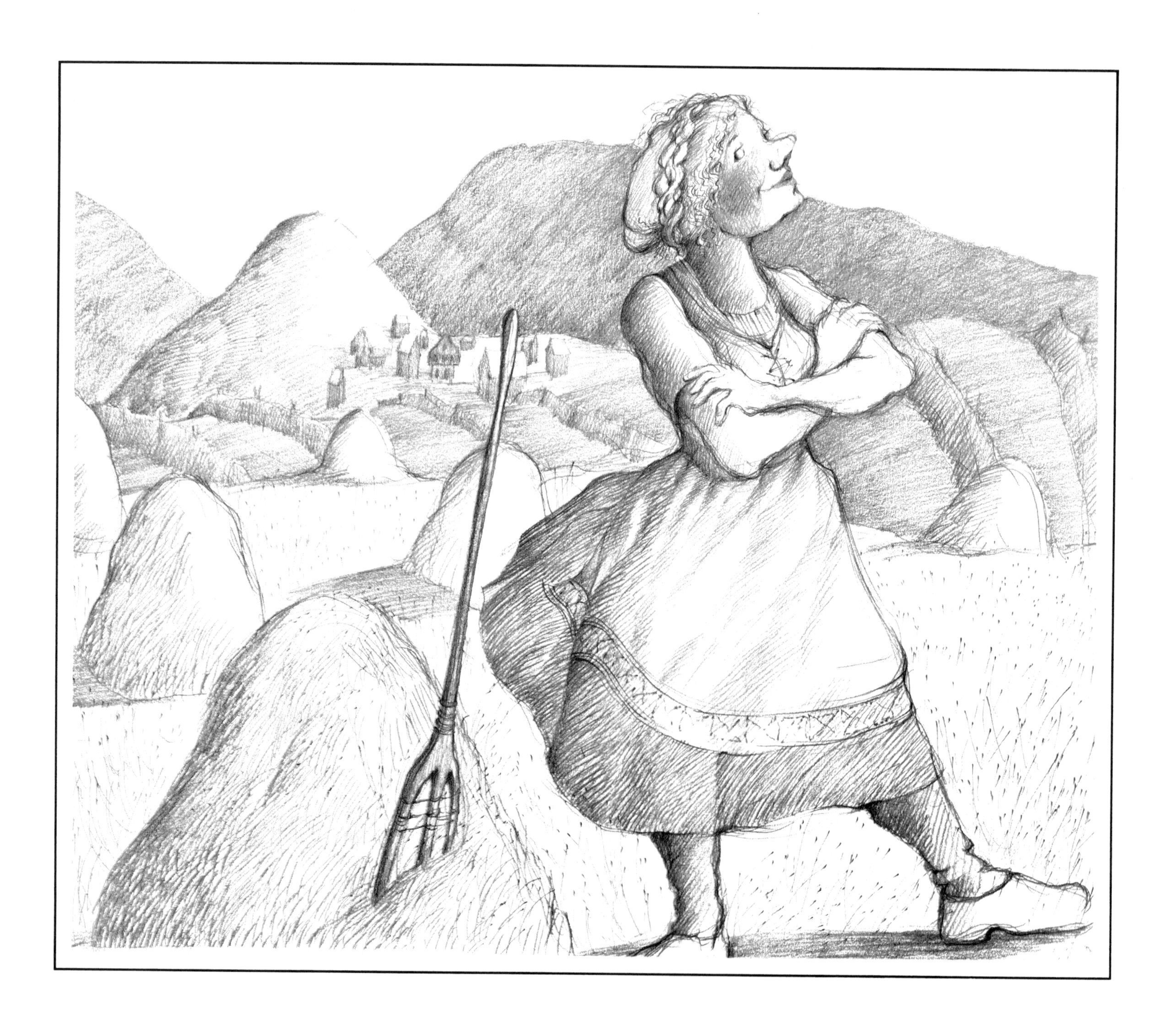

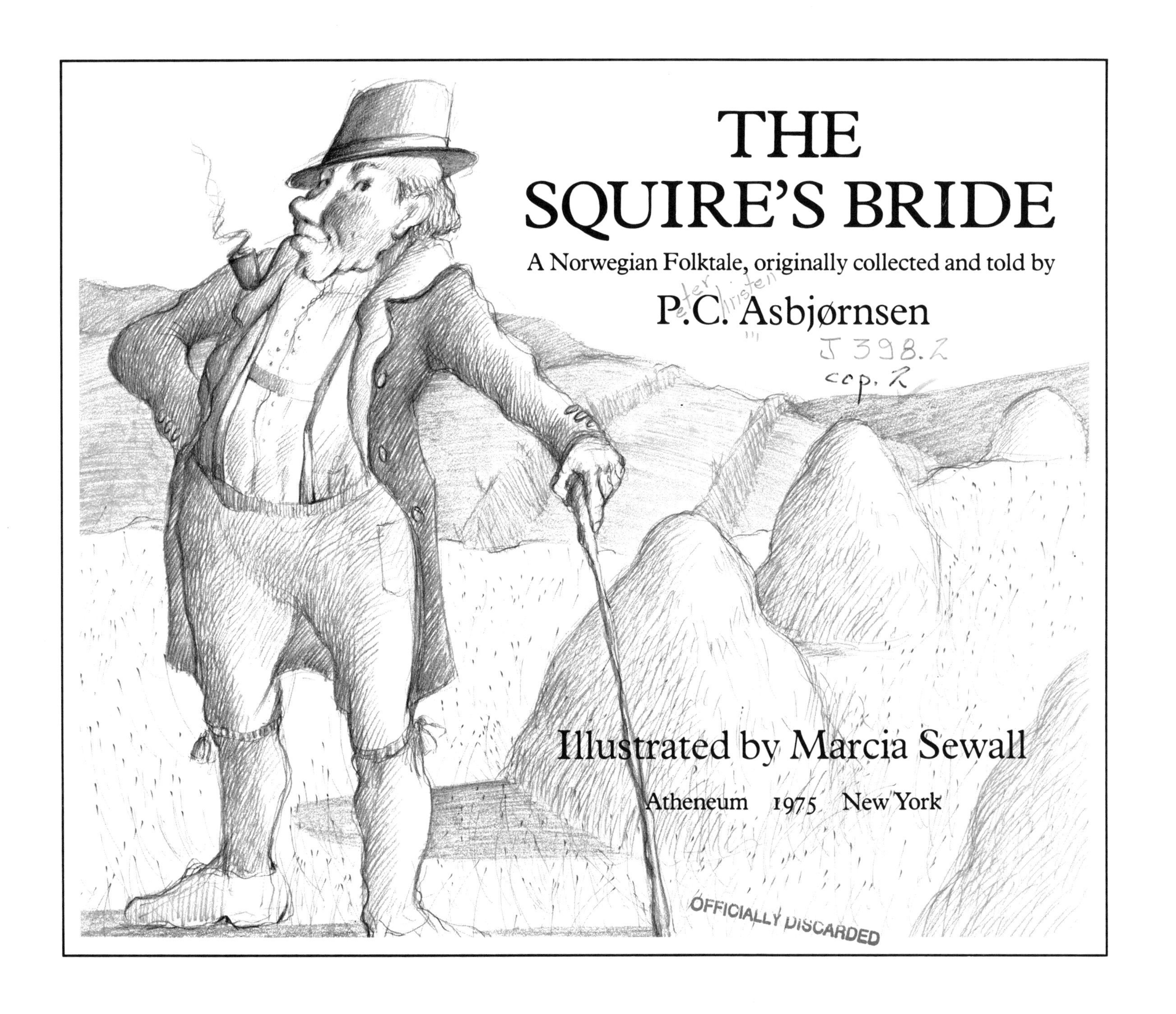

THE SQUIRE'S BRIDE

A Norwegian Folktale, originally collected and told by

P.C. Asbjørnsen

Illustrated by Marcia Sewall

Atheneum 1975 New York

Library of Congress Cataloging in Publication Data
The Squire's bride.
SUMMARY: *The old widower squire is determined to marry the farmer's daughter who is equally determined he will not.*
[1. Folklore—Norway] I. Sewall, Marcia, illus.
PZ8.1.S776 398.2'2'09481 [E] 74-19316
ISBN *0-689-30463-3*

English version based on a translation by H. L. Brækstad

Published simultaneously in Canada by
McClelland & Stewart Ltd.
Manufactured in the United States of America
Printed by Connecticut Printers Inc., Hartford
Bound by A. Horowitz & Son/Bookbinders
Clifton, New Jersey
First edition

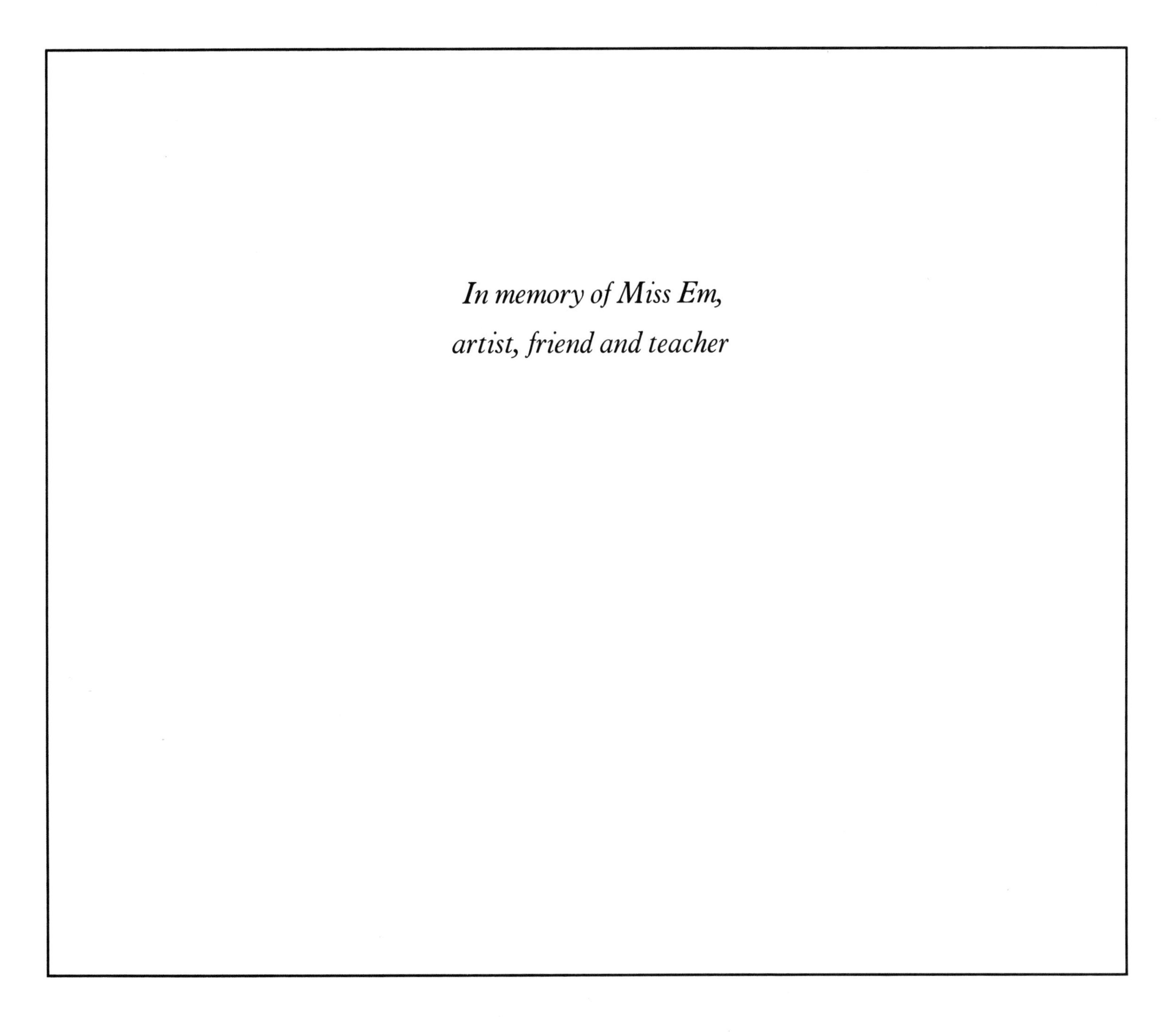

In memory of Miss Em,
artist, friend and teacher

Once upon a time there was a rich squire who owned a large farm, and had plenty of silver at the bottom of his chest, and money in the bank besides. But he felt there was something wanting; for his wife was dead and he was alone.

One day the daughter of a neighboring farmer was working for the squire in his hayfield. The squire saw her and liked her very much; and since she was the child of poor parents, he thought if he only hinted at the fact that he wanted her, she would be ready to marry him at once.

So he told her he had been thinking of getting married again.

"Ay! one may think of many things," said the girl, laughing slyly. She really thought the old fellow ought to be thinking of something better suited to his age than getting married.

"Well, you see, I thought that you should be my wife!"

"No, thank you all the same," said she, "that's not at all likely."

The squire was not used to being refused, and the more she said no, the more determined he was to marry her.

But try as he would he made no progress; so he sent for her father and said that if he could arrange the matter with his daughter, the debt he owed the squire would be forgiven and he would also get the piece of land that lay close to his meadow into the bargain.

"Well then, you may be sure I'll bring my daughter to her senses," said the father. "She is only a child, and she doesn't know what's best for her."

But all his coaxing and talking did not help matters. "I would not have the squire," she said, "if he sat buried in gold up to his ears!"

The squire waited day after day, and heard no more. At last he became so angry and impatient that he told the father he would have to put his foot down and settle the matter at once, for there was no waiting any longer.

The poor farmer saw nothing to do, but to let the squire get everything ready for the wedding; and when the parson and the wedding guests had arrived, the squire would send for the girl as if she were wanted for some work on the farm. When she came, she would be married right away, so that she would have no time to think it over.

The squire thought this was well and good; so he began brewing and baking and getting ready for the wedding in grand style.

Then when the day and the guests had arrived, the squire called one of his farm lads and told him to run down to his neighbor and ask him to send what he had promised.

"But if you are not back in a twinkling," the squire said, shaking his fist, "I'll – "

He did not say more; for the lad was off like a shot.

"My master has sent me to get what you promised him," said the lad, when he got to the neighbor. "There is no time to be lost, for he is terribly busy today."

"Yes, yes! Run down into the meadow and take her with you. There she goes!" answered the neighbor.

"The lad ran off, and when he came to the meadow, he found the daughter there raking the hay.

"I am to fetch what your father has promised my master," said the lad.

"Ah, ha!" thought she. "Is that what they are up to?"

"Ah, indeed!" she said. "I suppose it's that little bay mare of ours. You had better go and take her. She stands there tethered on the other side of the pea field."

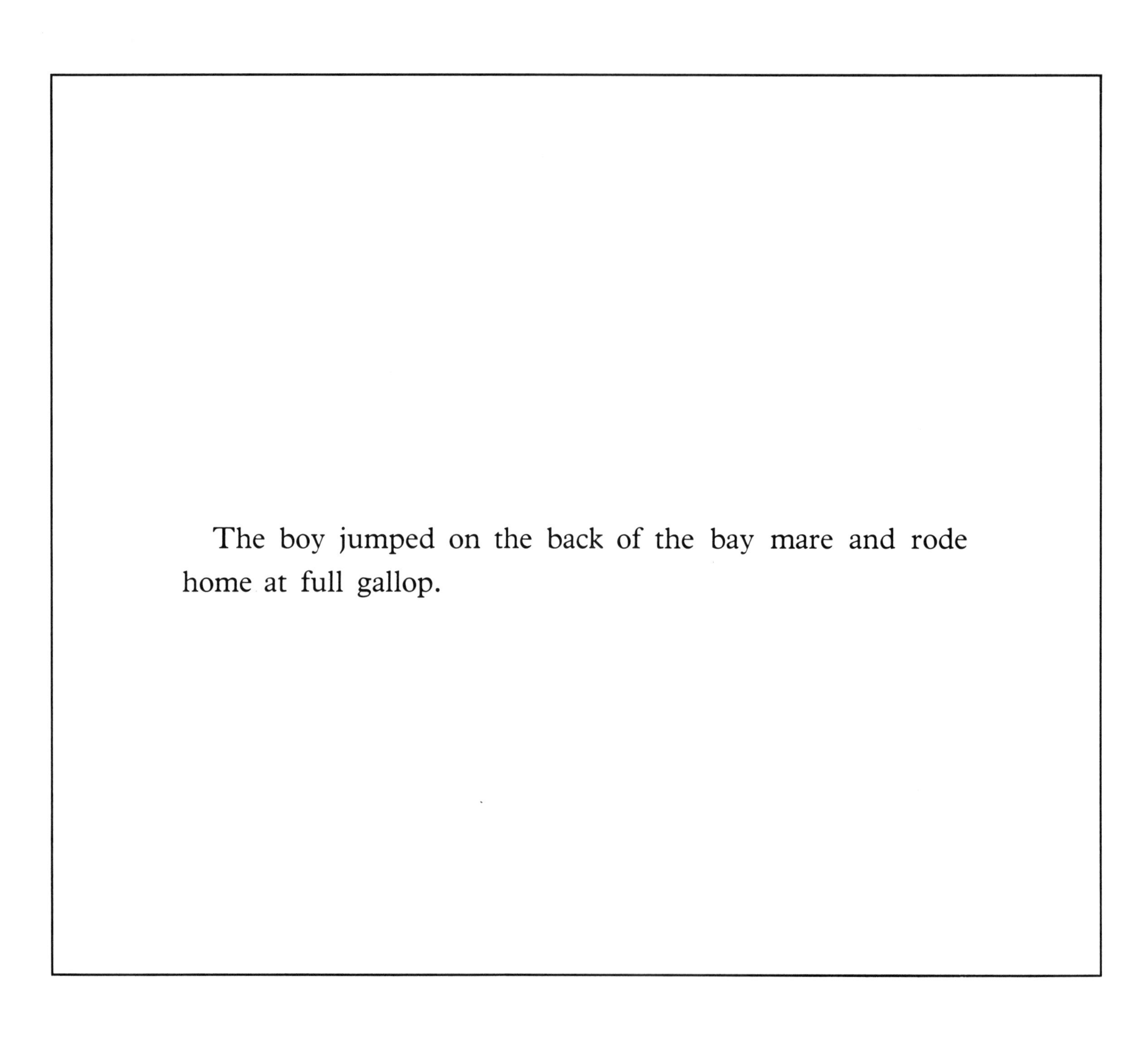

The boy jumped on the back of the bay mare and rode home at full gallop.

"Have you got her with you?" asked the squire.

"She is down at the door," said the lad.

"Take her up to the room my mother had," said the squire.

"But, master, how can that be managed?" said the lad.

"Just do as I tell you," said the squire. "If you cannot manage her alone, then get the men to help you," he added, for he thought the girl might be stubborn.

When the lad saw his master's face, he knew it would be no use to say anything more. So he went and got all the farm tenants who were there to help him. Some pulled at the head and the forelegs of the mare, and others pushed from behind, and at last they got her up the stairs and into the room.

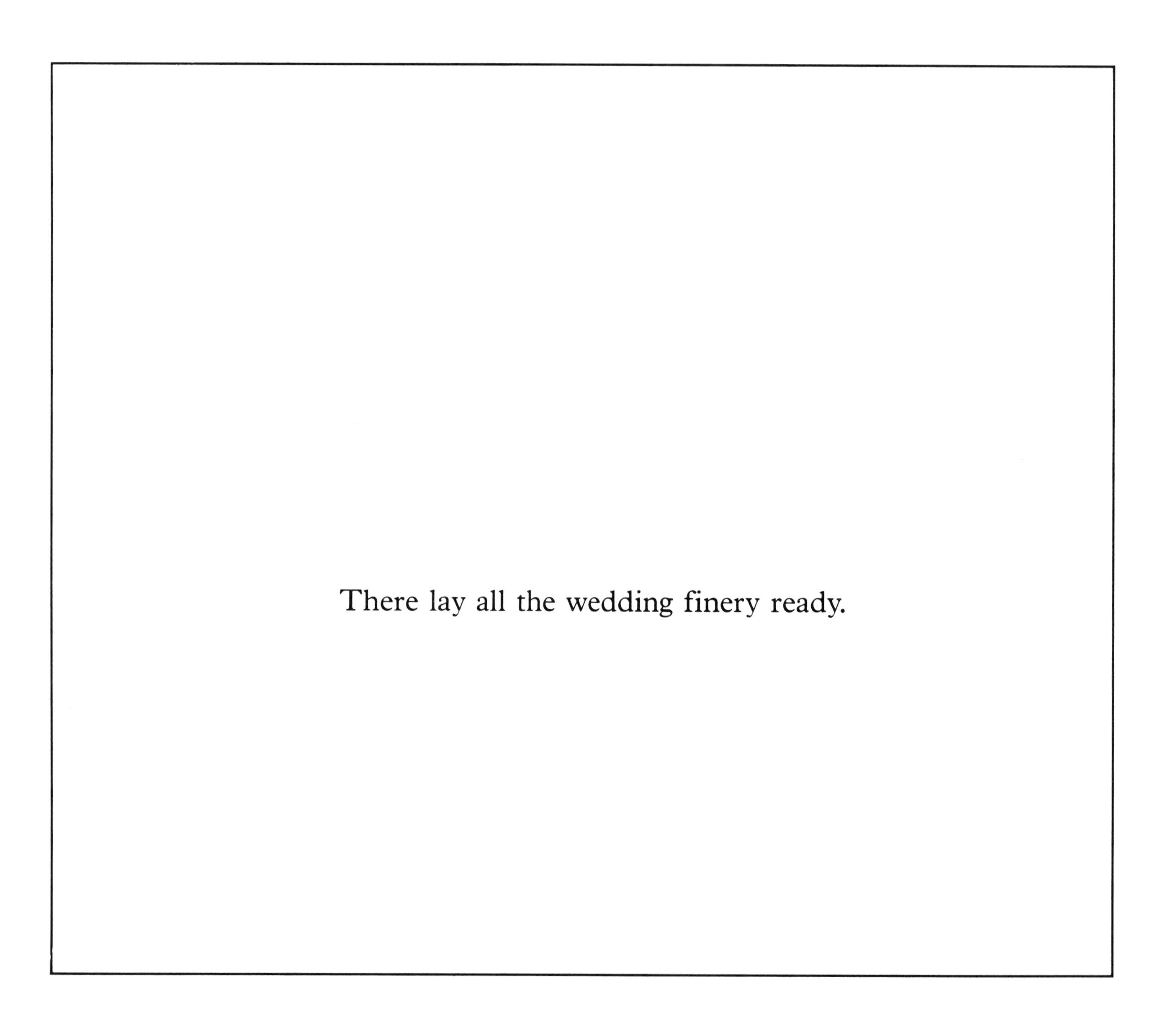

There lay all the wedding finery ready.

"Now, that's done, master!" said the lad; "but it was a terrible job. It was the worst thing I have ever had to do here on the farm."

"Never mind, you shall not have done it for nothing," said his master. "Now send the women up to dress her.

"But I say, master–!" said the lad.

"None of your talk!" said the squire. "Tell them they must dress her, and mind that they not forget either the wreath or the crown."

The lad ran into the kitchen.

"Look here, lasses," he said; "you must go upstairs and dress the bay mare as a bride. I expect the master wants to give the guests a laugh.

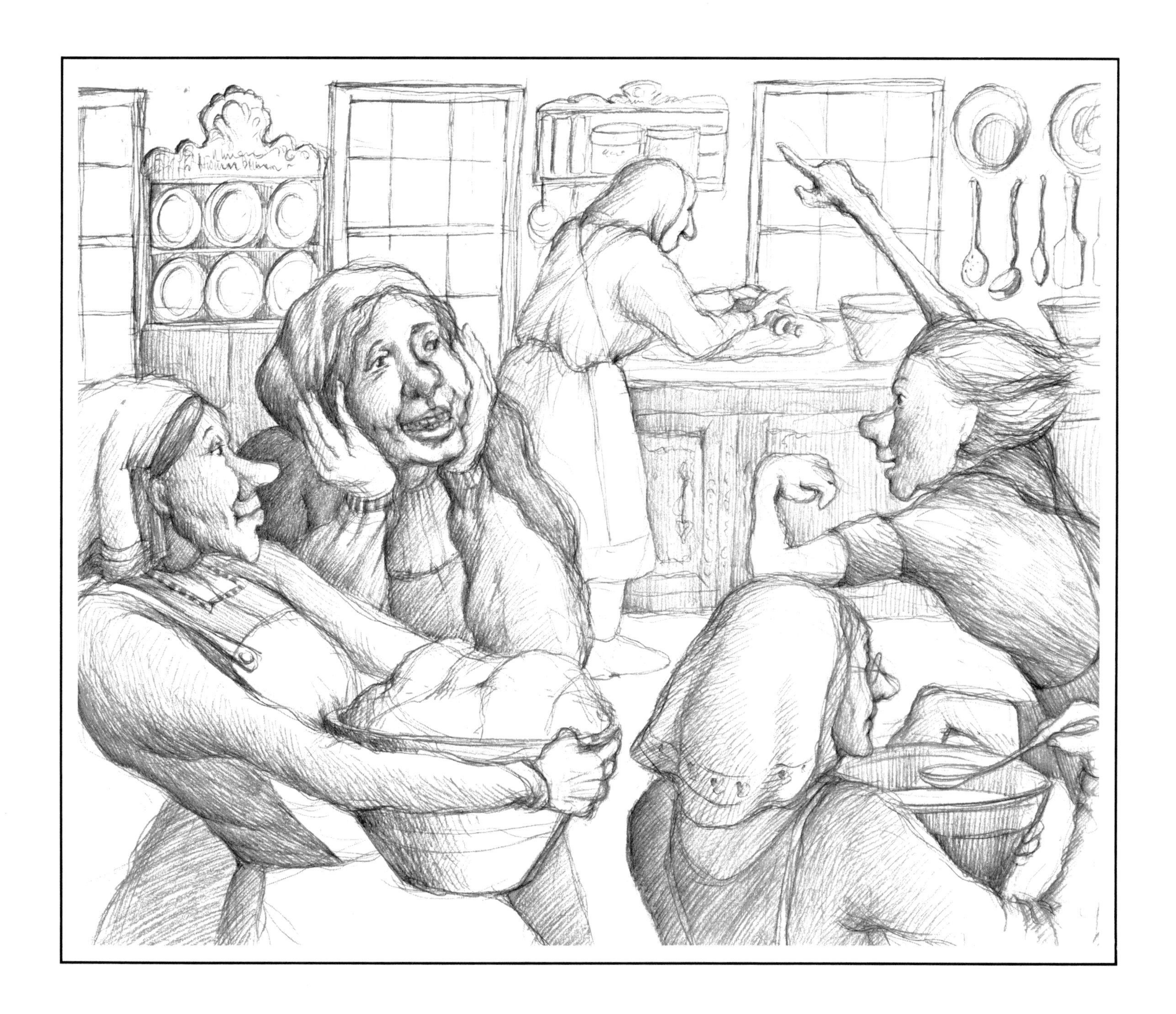

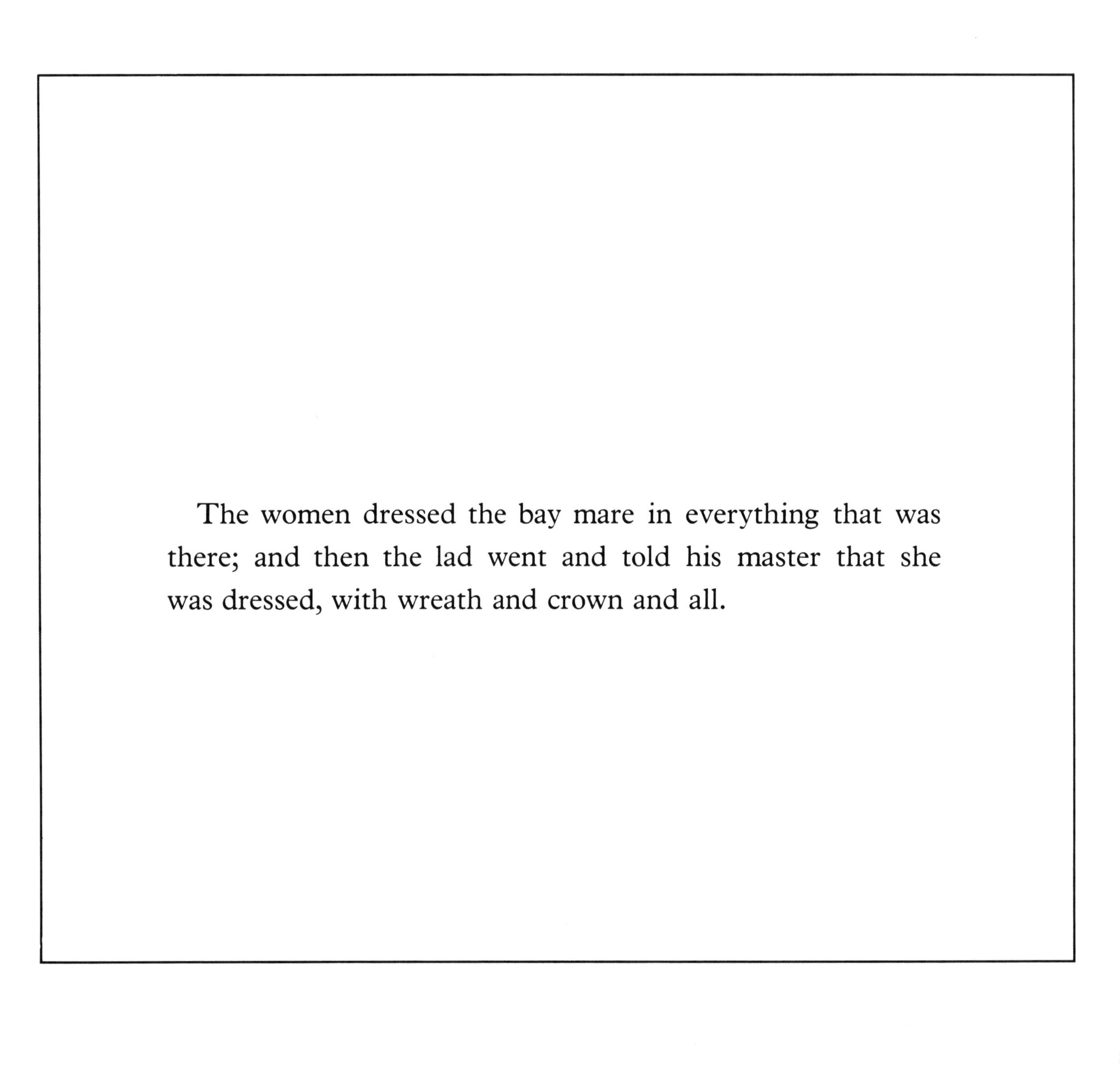

The women dressed the bay mare in everything that was there; and then the lad went and told his master that she was dressed, with wreath and crown and all.

"Very well, bring her down!" said the squire. "I will receive her myself at the door," said he.

There was a terrible clatter on the stairs; for that bride, as you know, had no silken shoes on.

When the door was opened and the squire's bride entered the parlor, you can imagine there was a good deal of tittering and grinning.

And as for the squire, you may be sure he had had enough of that bride, and they say he never went courting again.